**This book is to be returned on or before
the last date stamped below.**

For David with love – M.R.
For Ruth with love – B.C.

Text copyright © 2001 Margaret Ryan
Illustrations copyright © 2001 Ben Cort

Published in Great Britain in 2001
by Hodder Wayland, an imprint of
Hodder Children's Books

The right of Margaret Ryan to be identified as the
author of this Work and the right of Ben Cort to be identified
as the illustrator of this Work has been asserted by them in
accordance with the Copyright, Designs and Patents Act 1988.

British Library Cataloguing in Publication Data
Ryan, Margaret, 1944 -
Harry and the Tiger
1. Harry (Fictitious character) – Juvenile fiction 2. Spring
- Juvenile fiction 3. Children's stories
I. Title
823.9'14 [J]

ISBN: 0 7502 3615 9

Printed in Hong Kong by Wing King Tong

Hodder Children's Books
A division of Hodder Headline Limited
338 Euston Road, London NW1 3BH

MARGARET RYAN

Harry and the Tiger

Illustrated by Ben Cort

HODDER
Wayland

an imprint of Hodder Children's Books

Harry's class were going to visit a farm.
"What animals will we see on the
farm?" asked their teacher, Mrs Brown,
as they got on the school minibus.

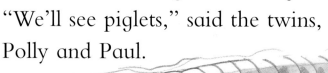

"We'll see lambs," said Lucy.
"We'll see ducklings," said Raj.
"We'll see piglets," said the twins,
Polly and Paul.

But Harry had other ideas.
"We'll see tigers," he said.

"Don't be silly, Harry," said Mrs
Brown. "Tigers don't live on farms."
Harry made a grumpy face.
He liked tigers.

"Now," went on Mrs Brown. "We know a song about a farm. Let's sing Old McDonald."

Lucy sang about lambs saying BAA BAA here and BAA BAA there, on Old McDonald's farm.

Raj sang about ducklings saying QUACK QUACK here and QUACK QUACK there, on Old McDonald's farm.

Polly and Paul sang about piglets saying OINK OINK here and OINK OINK there, on Old McDonald's farm.

But Harry sang about tigers saying
PURR PURR here and PURR PURR
there, on Old McDonald's farm.

"Don't be silly, Harry," said Mrs Brown. "Tigers don't purr."

Harry made another grumpy face. He liked tigers.

Soon they got to the farm. Lucy ran off to find the lambs. Raj ran off to find the ducklings. Polly and Paul ran off to find the piglets.

But Harry ran off to find the farmer.

He was in the big shed, mending the
tractor.

"Hello," said Harry. "Are you Old
McDonald, and do you have any tigers
on your farm?"

The farmer laughed and wiped his hands on an oily rag.

"I'm Farmer Jones," he said, "and it's funny you should ask about tigers. I do have some on the farm. Come and I'll show you."

Harry made a smiley face. He liked tigers.
Farmer Jones took him to the old barn,
and showed him the tigers.

"They're very small tigers," he said.
"You can stroke them if you like."
Harry stroked the tigers' soft fur.
Then he had an idea.

19

"Can I take one to surprise Mrs Brown?"
he asked.

"Certainly," said Farmer Jones.

When Harry found Mrs Brown she was in the middle of the farmyard, in the middle of all the children. They were talking about what they liked best on the farm.

"I liked the lambs best," said Lucy.
"Especially when they skipped about
saying, 'BAA BAA, where's my ma?' "

"I liked the ducklings best," said Raj. "Especially when they swam around saying, 'QUACK QUACK, where's my snack?' "

"We liked the piglets best," said Polly and Paul. "Especially when they trotted around saying, 'LOOK OUT, LOOK OUT, here comes my snout!'"

Then Harry said, "I liked the tigers best. Especially when they said, 'PURR PURR, stroke my fur.'"

"Don't be silly, Harry," sighed Mrs
Brown. "Tigers don't live on farms and
they don't purr."

"This one does," grinned Harry, and
out of his anorak he took a stripy kitten.

"Meet Tiger, everyone," he said. And he stroked her fur and she purred and purred.

"Well I never," laughed Mrs Brown.
"You weren't so silly after all, Harry."

Harry made a huge smiley face. He liked all kinds of tigers. Especially little ones!

Follow Harry through all four seasons, in these exciting Bright Star Books by Margaret Ryan:

Harry Keeps His Cool

It's Summertime, and Harry's feeling hot hot hot! He's in the garden with his family, finding ways to have fun. Now he's got hold of the garden hose . . . Oh no! Don't do that, Harry!

Tidy Up, Harry!

It's Autumn time, and Harry's sweeping up leaves and collecting apples. It's very hard work. But Harry has forgotten that Autumn leaves make bonfires and apples make toffee apples . . . Maybe Autumn's going to be fun after all!

Harry's Footprints

It's Winter time, and Harry wants to be the first to stamp his footprints in the snow. But can he put on his gloves, coat and boots before the rest of the family get out there too?

All these Bright Stars can be purchased from your local bookseller. For more information about Bright Stars, write to:
The Sales Department,
Hodder Children's Books,
338 Euston Road,
London NW1 3BH